Are You Ready for Bed?

For Olaf, with love
−Gaby Hansen

ISBN 0-439-58712-3

Text copyright © 2002 by Jane Johnson. Illustrations copyright © 2002 by Gaby Hansen.
All rights reserved. Published by Scholastic Inc., 557 Broadway, New York, NY 10012,
by arrangement with Tiger Tales, an imprint of ME Media, LLC. SCHOLASTIC and
associated logos are trademarks and/or registered trademarks of Scholastic Inc.

12 11 10 9 8 7 6 5 4 3 2 1   3 4 5 6 7 8/0

Printed in the U.S.A.   40

First Scholastic printing, November 2003

Are You Ready for Bed?

by Jane Johnson

Illustrated by Gaby Hansen

SCHOLASTIC INC.

New York Toronto London Auckland Sydney
Mexico City New Delhi Hong Kong Buenos Aires

Mrs. Rabbit sighed when all of her children were tucked safely into bed. "Ah, peace and quiet at last," she said.

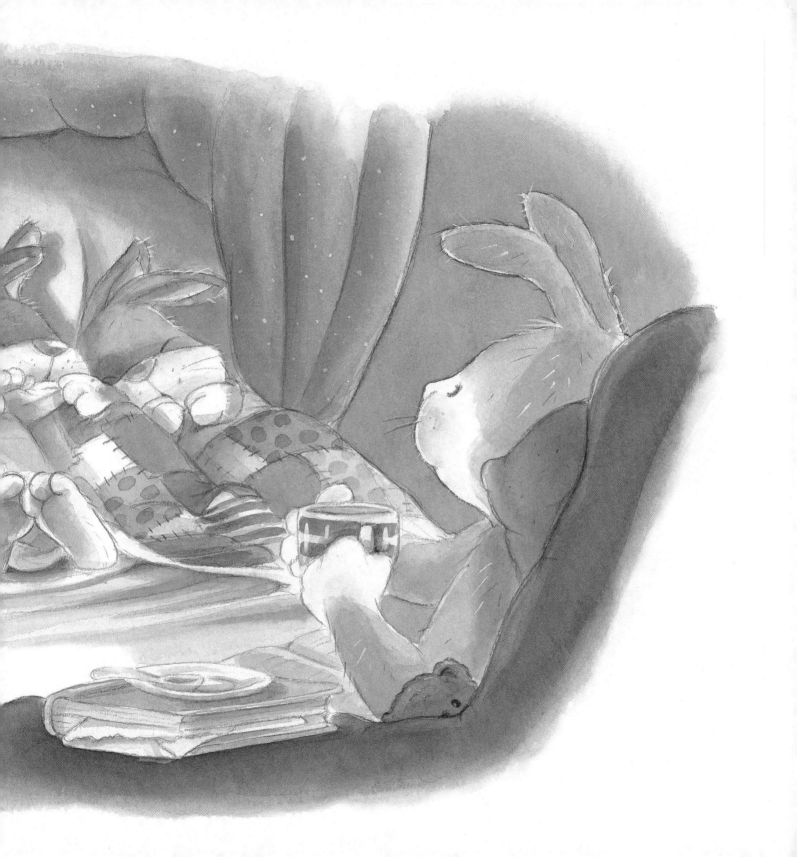

But Mrs. Rabbit had spoken too soon.

"Mommy, I can't sleep," said her youngest child,
Little Bunny, interrupting her first snore.

Mrs. Rabbit tried a gentle lullaby.

"Hush-a-bye bunny on the tree top,

When the bough breaks, the cradle . . ."

Little Bunny's eyes began to close.

"Is my bunny sleepy now?" whispered Mrs. Rabbit,

so as not to wake the others.

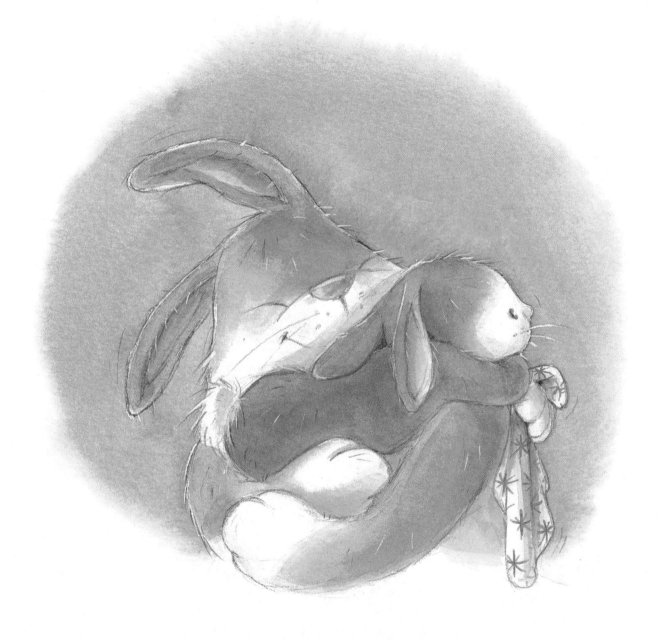

"No!" said Little Bunny. "I'm not sleepy
at all." He wanted to stay up all night long
with his mommy.

Mrs. Rabbit tried a bubble bath.

"Rub-a-dub dub, my bunny needs a scrub," she laughed.

"Who's my Little Bunny?"

"I am!" Little Bunny said, smiling sweetly.

"Well now, darling, I think it's bedtime,"
Mrs. Rabbit said hopefully, drying his fur.

"No!" said Little Bunny. "It's not bedtime yet."

Mrs. Rabbit tried warm milk.

"Swirly, whirly, creamy white," she yawned.

"Time to cuddle and say 'Good night.'"

"Cuddle, yes! 'Good night,' no!" said
Little Bunny. He wanted stay up with
his mommy forever.

"Squeezy, huggy, snuggle up tight," he said happily. "Am I the best little bunny in the world tonight?"

"I love all my bunnies the same, sleepyhead," said Mrs. Rabbit.

"Then I'll never be ready for bed,"
said Little Bunny.

"What am I going to do with you?"
said his worn-out mother. Little Bunny
jumped up excitedly…

"Let's play bunny hops!"
said Little Bunny.

"Hoppity, hoppity, hop…

'round and 'round the
room till I…"

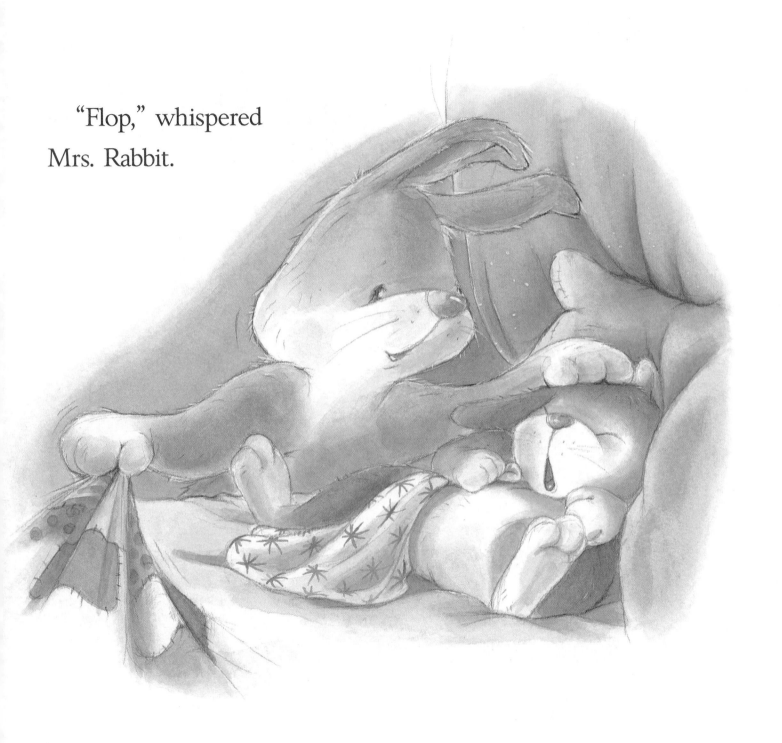

"Flop," whispered
Mrs. Rabbit.

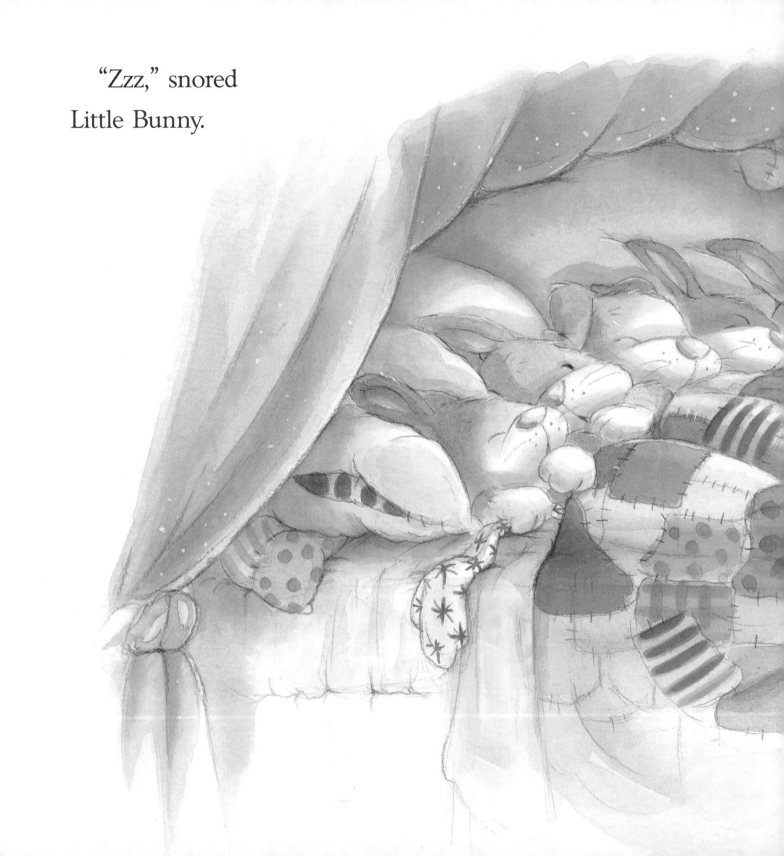

"Zzz," snored
Little Bunny.

"Ah, peace and quiet at last," sighed
Mrs. Rabbit. "Even my youngest bunny
is asleep in bed."

Mrs. Rabbit flopped into
bed, but through her
snores she heard...

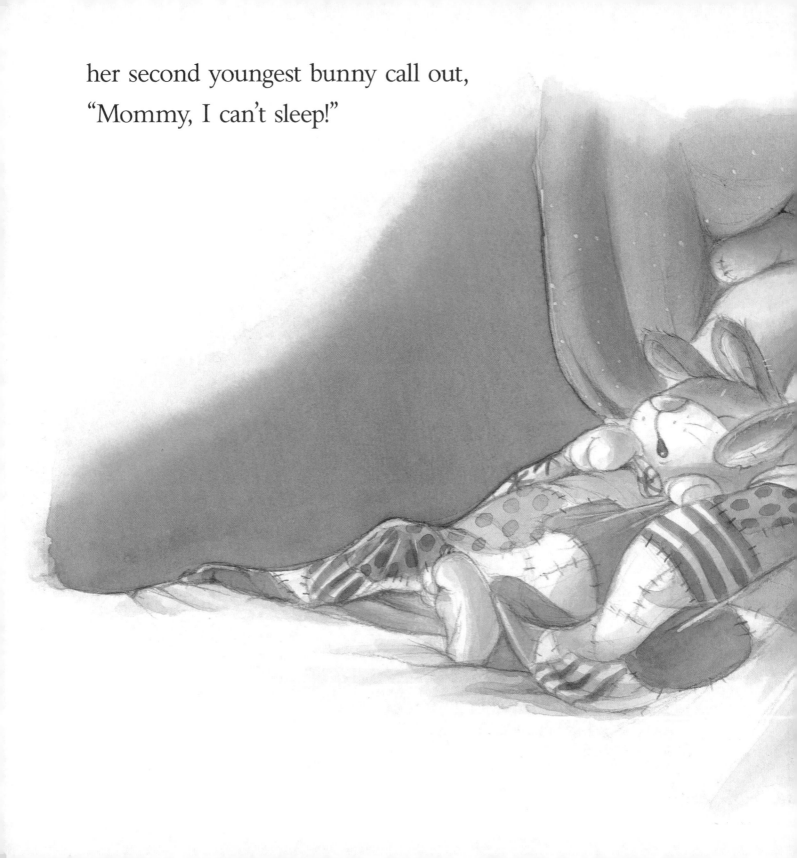

her second youngest bunny call out,
"Mommy, I can't sleep!"